TRACK 6

Fold Your Petals Up

We are the daisies, we are the
  'day's eye'
We open our eye to gaze at
  the sun
Cheery and simple, the
  flower of children
We close our eye when the
  day is done
So fold your petals up, wish wish
  wish wish, and close your eye

Hi! We're hibiscus, colourful and
  fabulous
We open to put on a show each day
For the insect crowd, who leave in
  the evening
Then delicately fold our petals away
So fold your petals up, wish wish
  wish wish, and close your eye

When night falls there's no reason
  to stay open
The sun will rise again by and by
The bees and the butterflies have all
  gone home
So fold your petals up, wish wish
  wish wish, and close your eye

We are the sunflowers and when we
  were buds
We followed the sun crossing the sky
From east in the morning to west in
  the evening
Then back in the night, to be standing
  by
So fold your petals up, wish wish
  wish wish, and close your eye

We are the poppies, on tall slender
  stems
Glowing in colours pure and bright
Scarlet in Flanders, gold in California
Silken flags in the twilight
Ooooo wish wish wish wish

When night falls there's no reason
  to stay open
The sun will rise again by and by
The bees and the butterflies have all
  gone home
So fold your petals up, wish wish
  wish wish, and close your eye

TRACK 7

Hibernatin'

Hibernatin' in my cosy den
through the long cold winter
I been waitin' since I don't know when
through the long cold winter
While the gales an' the blizzards blow
my body is set on slow
but I'm not frozen
I'm just dozin'
Dozin', waitin', hibernatin',
hi-ber–nat-in' . . .

Ooougghhhh . . .

Hibernatin' in my cosy den
through the long cold winter
I been waitin' since I don't know when
through the long cold winter
While I'm in hibernation
oblivious to creation
in my coat of fur
I will not stir
till my little body clock
goes knock knock knock
in the snow-meltin', twig-buddin',
  bud-poppin', sun-shinin',
green an' delicious
Spring!

TRACK 8

I Pianeti
(The Planets)

When I look up to
  the sky at night
I see you, tiny dots of light
Le-li-li-li, li-li-li-li-li, lay-lay-lay-lay,
  lay-lay-lay-lay
Nonno says you are vast
and I am the tiny one
Yet we circle around our sun
circle round together

il Sole is circled by Mercurio
Venere then la Terra
Marte, Giove, Saturno
Urano e Nettuno
They circle around our sun
and we circle round together

Each planet stays in its proper place
in our sistema solare
Le-li-li-li, li-li-li-li-li, lay-lay-lay-lay,
  lay-lay-lay-lay
Nonno says you are vast
and I am the tiny one
Yet we circle around our sun
circle round together

il Sole is circled by Mercurio
Venere then la Terra
Marte, Giove, Saturno
Urano e Nettuno
They circle around our sun
and we circle round together

Nonno says you are vast
and I am the tiny one
Yet we circle around our sun
circle round together

TRACK 9

It Will All Be There
Tomorrow

Day is done, sleep little one
It will all be there tomorrow
Scattered shells, sand in your toes
It will all be there

Feel the waves lift and sway
Gently rocking, rocking you, child
Like a little boat, go drifting away
Gently rocking, rocking you

We are the sea and the wind and
  the rain
With our lullaby for you, child
Through the night our soft refrain
Ooooooooo

Hear the rain, the steady drum
Falling down 'n' down 'n' down
  'n' down all over
Blessed again, with the drone and
  the hum
And the murmur of the river

We are the sea and the wind and
  the rain
With our lullaby for you, child
Through the night our soft refrain
Ooooooooo

Hush little one, hear the wind play
Sighing through the trees
Hush little one, hear the lullaby
On the evening breeze
Close your eyes

Hear the sea flow
Hear the wind
Hear the rain
Let the day go

I'm still awake, still!

Story and songs by
Elizabeth Honey & Sue Johnson

ALLEN&UNWIN

For Rosalind
E.H.

For Allegra and Miro
S.J.

First published in 2008

Allen & Unwin
83 Alexander St
Crows Nest NSW 2065
Australia
Phone: (61 2) 8425 0100
Fax: (61 2) 9906 2218
Email: info@allenandunwin.com
Web: www.allenandunwin.com

National Library of Australia
Cataloguing-in-Publication entry:
Honey, Elizabeth, 1947- .
I'm still awake, still!
ISBN 978 1 74175 321 9.
1. Bedtime – Juvenile fiction.
2. Wakefulness – Juvenile fiction.
I. Johnson, Sue. II. Title.
A823.3.

Cover design by Elizabeth Honey and Ruth Grüner
Text design by Ruth Grüner
Set in 18 pt Adobe Caslon Antique by Ruth Grüner
Illustrated in gouache
Printed in China by Everbest Printing Co. Ltd

10 9 8 7 6 5 4 3 2 1

In a cherry-coloured house
with an upstairs
and a downstairs
lived Marlo, Parlo, Nonno
and Fiddy.

Fiddy was small and busy and quick. When he had a bath at the end of the day there'd be dipping and diving and splishing and splashing and crocodiles and boats until Marlo said, 'Time for bed now, little Fiddy.'

'But I'm not tired,' said Fiddy.

'Ooo, soft new pyjamas,' said Marlo. 'Cosy and warm for drifting and dreaming.'

Marlo read Fiddy a story, then she turned down the light and sang softly,
'Goodnight my little darling, goodnight my little one.'

When Fiddy was quiet Marlo tip-toed out of the room.

'I'm still awake, still!'
called Fiddy.

'Not tired, little Fiddy?' said Parlo.
'When I can't sleep I dream up
something wondrous and sing about it
in my head. Try that, little Fiddy.'

Then he tucked him in and

kissed him goodnight.

Fiddy sang about his new pyjamas. 'I am the land all covered in rainbows . . . Goodnight orange and yellow, goodnight ruby red, green, blue, indigo and violet, all covering me.'

'Hey . . .' called Fiddy.

'I'm still awake, still.

And so is monkey.'

But Marlo, Parlo and Nonno were downstairs, dancing in the kitchen.

So Fiddy looked all around the room and he sang,
'Goodnight gumboots, goodnight jacket, goodnight Nonno's train ticket . . .'
And the gumboots danced with his jacket and the ticket danced a tickety jig.
And when he sang 'Goodnight Humpty, dump dumpty Humpty'
Humpty fell off the table – again!

Fiddy sang, 'Goodnight toy-box, monkeys and bears . . .'
And all the toys twirled and whooped and whirled.

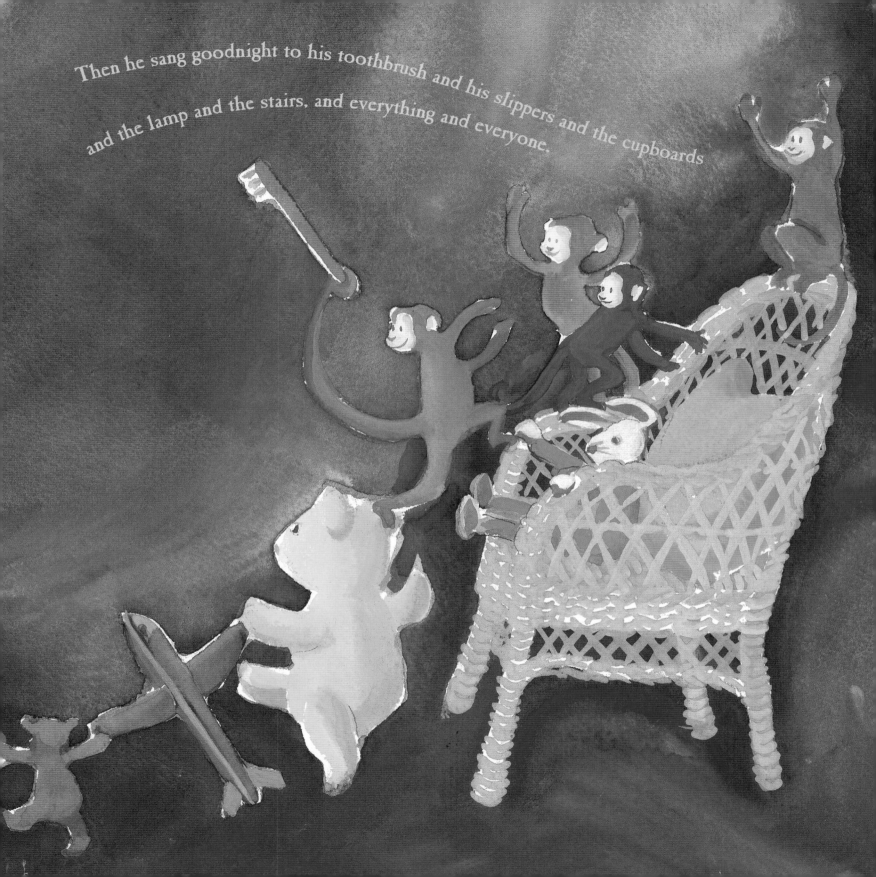

Then he sang goodnight to his toothbrush and his slippers and the cupboards and the lamp and the stairs, and everything and everyone.

'I'm still awake, still,'
called Fiddy.

Then a soft voice said,
'Who's still awake?'
It was a possum.

'Furry possum!'
cried Fiddy.
'How do you sleep?'
'I snooze all day
in a hollow tree,'
said the possum.
'Night time's the time
for climbing and leaping.'

'Want to know how I sleep?' said a drowsy little voice.

It was a baby koala.
    'I sleep piggyback on my mum.'
And a joey said,
    'I sleep in my mother's pouch.'
And the echidna said,
    'I dig in under a log.'
And a wombat snuffled,
    'I doze in my earthy burrow.
    How do *you* sleep, little human?'

'I don't know,' said Fiddy.
'I'm still awake, still.'

Then a silky voice said, 'Not sleepy?'

It was a poppy.

'Why don't you be like us?' said the poppy.
'Early in the morning when the sun comes up,
open out your petals and put on a show.'

'Buzz,' said a bee. 'Buzzzzzz.'

'Then in the evening when the sun goes down,' said the poppy,
'fold your petals up and close your eye. It's simple.'
'That's easy for flowers,' said Fiddy, 'but I don't have petals.'

Then a deep voice growled, 'What's the matter?'

It was a big friendly bear.

'I should be asleep,' said Fiddy, 'but I'm still awake, still.'

'Ooohh . . .' yawned the bear, 'nothing to fuss about, just let it happen . . .'

'Mmm . . . I feel like a snooze right now . . . mmm . . .'

'Bear!' said Fiddy, tugging his ear. 'Where do you sleep?'

'Grrroah . . .' groaned the bear. 'I hibernate in my cosy den.'

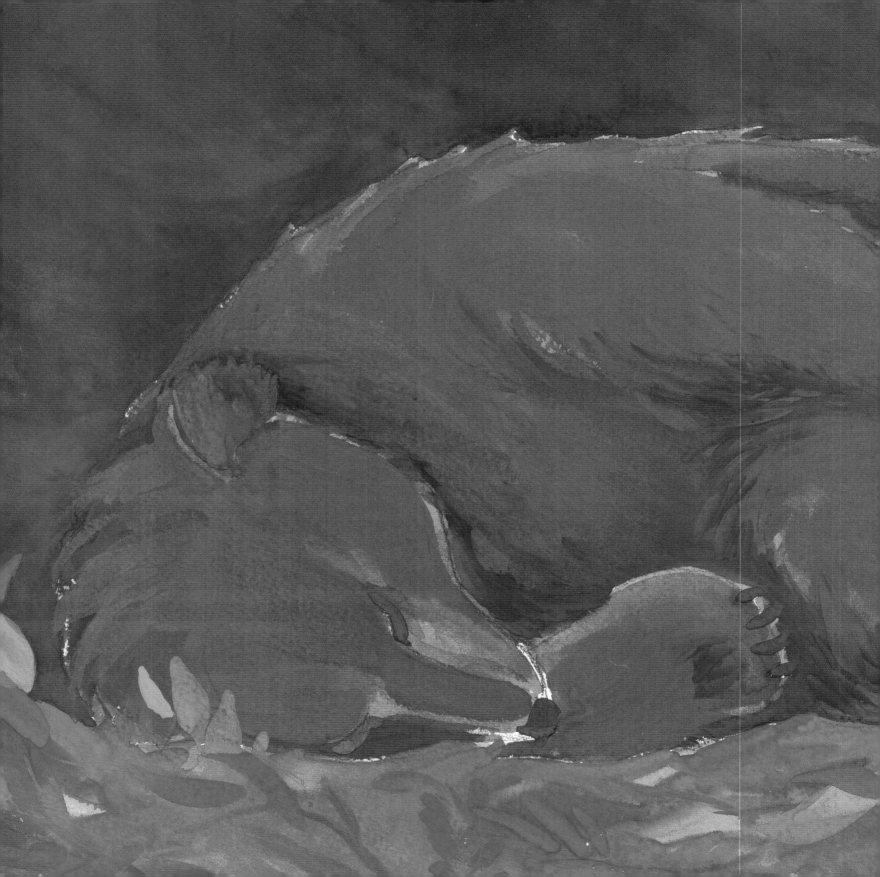

'Dozing, waiting, hibernating, till the green and delicious Spring.
Oooooooooaahh . . . .

Fiddy curled up and tried to hibernate.

'Oh, I'm still awake, still!'
Fiddy looked up at the twinkling stars
and remembered Nonno's favourite song.
'Nonno,' he called. '*Nonno!*'

'Fiddy!' said Nonno. 'Caro mio, what a restless boy.'
'Nonno, I need the song about the planets,' said Fiddy.
'Then sing it,' said Nonno.

'When I look up to the sky at night, I see you, tiny dots of light,' sang Fiddy.
'Nonno says you are vast and I am the tiny one . . .'

When Nonno joined in, he scooped Fiddy up and waltzed him back to bed.

As Nonno's deep voice sang, 'We circle around the sun and we circle round together'

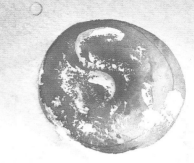

Fiddy floated like the planets in the song.

Fiddy yawned. 'I'm still . . .'

'Shhhhh,' whispered the breeze. 'Listen . . .'

Fiddy closed his eyes . . .

The whole world was singing softly,

and like a little boat he was drifting away . . . drifting . . . dreaming . . .

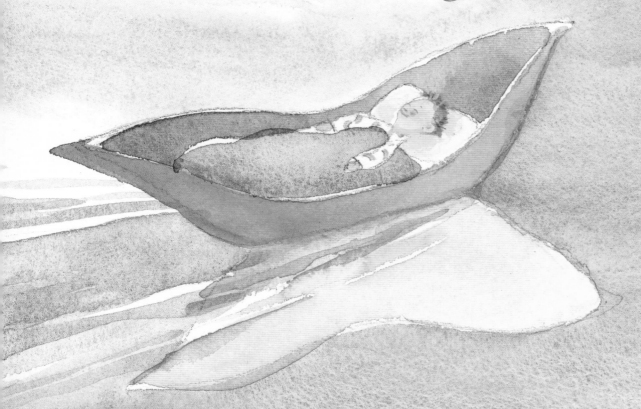

'Goodnight, Fiddy, goodnight.'

I'm still awake, still!
THE SONGS

Acknowledgements

With thanks to Rosalind Price, Hadyn Buxton, Sue Flockhart, The Johnson Family and also to Margaret Finch and the staff and children at Isabel Henderson Kindergarten.

Elizabeth Honey is an award-winning author of poetry, picture books and novels. Her playful humour, originality and energy strike a chord with children everywhere. Elizabeth is also an artist and she illustrates her own books. Her picture books include *The Moon in the Man* and *Not a Nibble!* Her novels are published in many countries.

The first song by Elizabeth Honey and Sue Johnson, 'All the Wild Wonders', was nominated for the 2003 APRA Music Awards.

Sue Johnson is a singer, pianist and composer. She is also co-founder of the internationally renown vocal percussion group Coco's Lunch. Sue's original songs have been performed and recorded in Australia, Canada and USA. She has composed for television, film and dance, and has led vocal workshops and directed massed choirs. Sue is an inspirational teacher and choirs sing her praise.

Coco's Lunch have two CDs for children: *Wally Wombat Shuffle* and *Rat Trap Snap!*, which was nominated for an Aria Award for Best Children's Album in 2007.

Visit the website for Coco's Lunch www.cocoslunch.com

I'm still awake, still!
Original songs by Elizabeth Honey & Sue Johnson
Copyright © Lyrics, Elizabeth Honey 2008
Copyright © Composition and arrangements, Sue Johnson 2008

1. **Story read by Elizabeth Honey,** including songs 33.36
2. **Goodnight My Little Darling** 2.51
3. **My Rainbow Pyjamas** 2.54
4. **Goodnight Gumboots** 2.29
5. **Furry Little Possum** 4.01
6. **Fold Your Petals Up** 3.31
7. **Hybernatin'** 2.56
8. **I Pianeti (The Planets)** 3.57
9. **It Will All Be There Tomorrow** 4.33

TOTAL RUNNING TIME 60.50

SUE JOHNSON *voice, piano, accordion*
ELIZABETH HONEY *narration*
MARK JOHNSON *voice, hybernatin' bear, possum, gumboots*
GABRIELLE MacGREGOR *voice, flower chorus*
NICOLA EVELEIGH *voice, flower chorus*
SEBASTIANO LO BARTOLO *voice, grandfather*
KIRSTY GREIG *violin*
SARAH CUMING *cello*
LIZ FRENCHAM *double bass*
ALEX PERTOUT *congas, cabasa*

Produced by Sue Johnson

Co-produced, engineered and mixed by Hadyn Buxton

Recorded at Hadyn Buxton Studio and Newmarket Studio

Music mastered by Ross Cockle at Sing Sing

Melbourne Australia